CW01021266

BOTH
PUBLISHING

First published on Tor.com.
Reprinted with permission of the Author.
This edition published in 2024 by BOTH Publishing

The author asserts their moral right to be
identified as the author of their work, in accordance
with the Copyright, Designs and Patents Act, 1988.

A CIP catalogue record of this book is available
from the British Library

ISBN - 978-1-913603-44-1

Printed by Ingram Spark.
Distributed by BOTH Publishing.

Cover art by Dion MBD.
Cover design by Chrissey Harrison and Alistair Sims.
Typeset by Chrissey Harrison.

Part of the Dyslexic Friendly Quick Reads Project.

www.booksonthehill.co.uk

THE NECESSARY ARTHUR

Garth Nix

Other dyslexic friendly quick read titles from BOTH publishing

Sharpe's Skirmish

Silver for Silence

Blood Toll

Anchor Point

The Dust of the Red Rose Knight

Snow in the Desert

Six Lights off Green Scar

Stamp of a Criminal

The Clockwork Eyeball

Sherlock Holmes and the Four
Kings of Sweden

The

Necessary Arthur

Tamara Tafika often came to the Sheepstones in summer, late in the long evenings, as the sun was sliding down all red into the west. The stone circle wasn't much, as stone circles went, nothing to rival Stonehenge or Avebury. There were only seven stones in all, and none were actually standing, the most upright of them leaning drunkenly at a sixty-degree angle, the others all long since succumbed to the horizontal.

The stones weren't that big either, the largest only five feet long and about two feet wide. They were limestone, brought a great distance in Bronze Age terms. A 1980s study had shown they likely came from western Yorkshire to their resting place here, just north of Hadrian's Wall. They had been roughly worked to give them some shape, but otherwise left undecorated.

Tamara liked to sit on the smallest stone and watch the sun slip away. It was a time for quiet contemplation, an escape from the pressure of her completed but not yet awarded PhD from the School of History, Classics and Archaeology at Newcastle University; and the usually greater or at least more annoying pressure from the undergraduate students she tutored.

Consequently she was a little annoyed this valuable time of solitude might be disturbed when she heard the swish and crackle of someone coming through the ferns that grew so thickly on the hillside, almost obscuring the track up from the layby off the road. She had parked her own car there, but she hadn't heard any traffic since.

The annoyance was coloured a little by caution. No one could see her from the road, so they wouldn't have stopped because they saw a single woman alone, and her car was the mud-splattered Land Rover her supervisor had lent her while he and his family were on vacation, also not suggestive of a lone female target. Even so, she held her big bunch of keys in her fist, with one ready to score across an attacker's face, just as she learned in self-defence classes. Better to be ready than not.

"A hundred fucking metres away! You did that on purpose."

It was a woman talking. Tamara relaxed a little, though not entirely, since it seemed the woman was talking to herself. Tamara could see her now, despite the fading light. A short, slight silver-haired woman in an almost luminously white double-breasted business suit, coming up the path in a series of tottering steps and near falls, which as she got closer, Tamara saw was due to extremely high shoes. Which had fluorescent blue-white heels.

"She could have put me down right next to you," complained the woman as she reached the stones. She was younger than Tamara had presumed from the sight of that silver hair. Close up and standing still rather than tottering on her six-inch heels, she looked a cool sixty rather than a doddering eighty.

"Er... she?" asked Tamara, meaning to humour this obviously batty old lady and depart as quickly as possible.

"Doesn't matter," declared the woman, with a wave of her hand. "Tamara Tafika."

"Um, yes," replied Tamara, even more mystified.

"Childhood in Lusaka, moved to UK with parents when you were three, Plymouth first, then Highgate; scholarships to excellent schools; parents died when you were sixteen, car crash, eccentric aunt made guardian but chose not to live with you; favourite food crumpets with Wilkin & Sons Tiptree

5

orange marmalade; you didn't break your wrist playing drunken croquet—"

"Er, no, I've never even played sober croquet and how would you break—"

"Undergraduate degree Cambridge in archaeology, starred first; favourite music a very obscure band called Harmmonius Drunk, awful music by the way; current, just completed postgraduate student Newcastle University, archaeology again. Newcastle both to be near the Wall, and to your aunt, right?"

"Yes, but—"

"Just data points," said the woman. She brushed off part of the stone near Tamara and sat down. "Got to make sure you're the right Tamara Tafika, right?"

"The right—"

"Enough with the rights. We've established who you are," said the woman. She shot her cuffs and looked at her watch, a tiny thing set with a great many diamonds. "Not a lot of time, is there? Ninety minutes to midnight, give or take."

"Look, I don't know how you know my—"

"Of course you don't," said the woman. "I'll explain as much as I can. Pointless really, since you won't remember at this stage, but still. The methodology must be followed. Not to mention abiding by the rules."

Tamara got up off the stone and started to edge away, keeping her eyes on the woman, ready for any sudden moves to attack or spit or whatever else she might take it into her head to do.

"Oh do stay still," said the woman. She waved her hand again, not dismissively, more like how a puppeteer might make a puppet jump.

Tamara stood still. She didn't mean to, she was trying to move her legs. But it was as if she was rooted to the earth. Strain as she might, she couldn't lift her feet from the ground.

"Now, first things first," said the woman. "You can call me Blaise."

"Like a fire?" asked Tamara, trying hard to keep the panic from her voice. She wasn't paralyzed, she could wiggle her toes and make her kneecaps go up and down, and wave her arms around. She just couldn't unstick her feet...

"No, B-l-a-i-s-e. Ess no zed."

"What... what do you want with me? Why can't I move my feet?"

"I am considering you for a position with my syndicate," said Blaise. "A very important position. According to my advisultants, you're the best candidate for this phase of the Game."

Tamara gulped several times, and forced herself to take as slow a breath as she could manage.

"What... what is an advisultant... and... candidate... Game?"

"Advisultant," said Blaise, tapping her temple twice. Her fingernails were painted the same fluorescent blue-white as her shoes. "Surely... oh... yes. Too soon. Well, that's not important either. Anyway, this mode of Game here on this world, is mythical, by region, and we're setting up our playing pieces. Right here, the most important of these, the absolutely necessary piece, will be an Arthur."

"A what?"

"An Arthur. You know, mythical king, joined all the warring parts of Britain into one kingdom. Excalibur, all that sort of stuff."

"King Arthur?"

"Yes, well, they don't need to be a king or a queen in this round of the game, obviously. It is the twenty-second... I mean twenty-first century."

"A woman can be Arthur?"

"Obviously," sighed Blaise. She narrowed her eyes to look at Tamara. "I am wondering..."

She tapped her temple again and gave a theatrical sigh.

"No... you are still the best candidate, believe it or not."

"You want *me* to be a... a... King Arthur?"

"Did I say that?" asked Blaise, nettled. "Arthur is a later stage piece, we couldn't play one now. We need you to be a Merlin. Didn't I say that?"

"No," replied Tamara. Her mouth hung open after the word, and she knew the expression on her face could only be what her mother had sometimes crossly described as 'classic village idiot'.

"Merlin," said Blaise. "You've got the potential, the connections. Very important piece in its own right, even if not Arthur. Precursor, you know. You'll have to identify Arthur in turn one, and take the baby away to a safe, defended place and oversee their education and all that, protect them, plus catalyse the revelation of their identity later—"

"No," said Tamara. "I don't know how you're sticking me here, but I'm not going to become your 'Merlin' and I am definitely not taking anyone's *baby*, and even if that wasn't enough I have my own life to live and—"

"It's not optional, dear," interrupted Blaise. "The stakes are too high for that."

"The... the stakes...?"

"Your world," explained Blaise. "Its future... oh, it's easier to show you. Look."

She pointed her finger at the air in front of her, which was instantly occupied by a howling, blinding, white-hot vortex.

"That's what happens if *They* win," said Blaise, wiggling her finger.

The vortex diminished to a small white dot that disappeared with a pinging noise.

"What… what happens if you win?" croaked Tamara, slowly lowering her hands from her ears.

"It's a lot better," reassured Blaise, though she made no move to show Tamara anything. "I mean most of the planet will still be around."

"Most of the—"

"So like I said, it's not optional. Now, we're in the pre-placement mode, time is of the essence. Turn one begins at midnight and the aggressors will doubtless use their free attack, so you have to be ready."

"Free attack—"

"One direct attack per turn," explained Blaise. "As opposed to preparation and so forth. *They* will be prepping something now, and they like to attack as swiftly as possible. So, are you clear on the mission?"

"No," replied Tamara.

"I wonder if everyone else is having the same trouble," muttered Blaise. "I should have swapped with whoever's got China, their Monkey candidate would have to be quicker on the uptake—"

"Just let me go!" yelled Tamara. She bent down and started to undo her boots, working on the theory that they were stuck to the ground and not her actual feet.

"Oh, stop fiddling about!"

Tamara stopped fiddling about. Crouched down, she found she could no longer do anything except breathe. Panic rose up in her, and she started to hyperventilate.

"And don't panic," instructed Blaise.

Tamara instantly felt calmer.

"Always good advice," added the old woman. "Let me reiterate. You are going to be our Merlin for this game, which consists of a number of turns, each of which is seven years. You will be opposed by *Them*, who will try and stop you reaching your objectives. Which are our objectives. To wit, you must locate the soon-to-be-born Arthur. You must spirit the baby away to a safe place, keep them safe, and arrange their education and eventual coming of age when they will assume their rightful place. The first twenty-four hours of every turn is the aggressor period. *They* can attack at any point in this twenty-four-hour period, but only once in turn one, twice in turn two, and three times in turn three and so on. Occasionally more in later turns, if certain precursor bonuses have been attained. Got that?"

Tamara made a noise in her throat.

"Oh, speak up!"

"Yes," said Tamara indignantly, regaining control over her own mouth. "But how exactly am I supposed to do any of this? I'm an archeologist, not some—"

"If you didn't interrupt me all the time I would have got to the point where I told you we'd be giving you the Knowledge and the Wand," said Blaise severely.

"The Knowledge?" asked Tamara, slightly hysterically. "Like a London taxi driver?"

"I believe that is a *very small* sub-section of *our* Knowledge," said Blaise. "Useful though. Particularly in the rain when you want to get to Claridge's from the Tower of London, and Upper Thames Street is being dug up like it was last week. But I digress."

She reached inside her suit jacket and pulled out something that looked like a blue Ventolin inhaler. Exactly like a Ventolin inhaler. She reached over and held it up to Tamara's ear.

"I'm not an asthmatic," said Tamara. "And if I was, surely my mouth—"

Blaise pushed the cylinder and a jet of intensely cold something pierced the inside of Tamara's ear and seemingly went straight through into the pain centres of her brain. She screamed and would have flung herself to the ground and curled into a ball, if she had been able to move.

For a moment, everything went black.

"It's not that bad," said Blaise. "Come on, pull yourself together. Had it myself numerous times. That's the Knowledge. It'll take a while to grow, though. You'll only have a few of the basics to start with."

"What?" sobbed Tamara. The pain was ebbing, but it still felt like the worst sinus headache she'd ever had. "Something's going to grow inside my head?"

"Only the Knowledge," said Blaise. "Information, wisdom, the sort of thing you might collect over the years anyway. Just much more of it, and a lot faster. And to be fair, a great deal currently unavailable on this benighted timeline."

"Timeline?"

"Oops," said Blaise. "So that's the Knowledge. Now, where did I put the Wand?"

She reached inside her suit jacket again, investigating more pockets than could actually be located there, before eventually nodding to herself and reaching inside her left sleeve. From that she drew out what appeared to be a plastic chopstick, though instead of Chinese characters advertising a restaurant printed on it, there were six or seven unfamiliar symbols.

"Moon powered," said Blaise. "You know."

"No…"

"Just make sure you leave it out somewhere when the moon is full, or near full, so it can lock on. You'll know how to use it once the Knowledge gets going. Go on, take it, it's yours."

"You've stuck me in this position," said Tamara, through gritted teeth.

"Oh, so I have," said Blaise. "Well, feel free."

Tamara tentatively straightened up, lifted one foot, and then the other. For a moment she contemplated swinging around and smacking Blaise in the head with her keys, but she knew that wouldn't help. The Knowledge was already at work, and though it had done little more than tell her how to begin to use the Wand, that was enough to confirm – if further confirmation was needed after she had been *immobilised* – that this all was really happening and she had no option but to go along with it.

"That's pretty much it," said Blaise. She handed the wand to Tamara, who took it, hefted it – it was much heavier than a plastic chopstick – and thrust it through her belt.

Blaise looked at her watch again. "Almost midnight."

"What!" exclaimed Tamara. She pulled

out her phone and checked the time. It was 11:58, and as per usual, there was no service. She looked around. The sun had set, and it was completely dark, except around the circle of standing stones, and that was only because Blaise's suit glowed like a fluorescent tube. "But it... it was only—"

"You fugued out for an hour," said Blaise. "Application of the Knowledge. But that's good. Imagine how painful it would be otherwise. And you didn't have any of the other side effects."

"What side effects?"

Blaise wasn't listening. She had her head up, as if she heard something. But there were no noises, save the very slight rustle of a light breeze in the ferns.

"Got to go," she said. "Good luck, Merlin."

Tamara didn't manage to do more than open her mouth before Blaise was gone.

She was there one instant, totally disappeared the next.

It was very, very dark.

The rustling in the ferns grew louder, more than could be explained by the breeze.

Tamara looked at her phone. It said 12:00.

She drew the wand, holding it in approved Harry Potter style, and directed its power as the Knowledge instructed her a mere second before an enormous grey-furred wolf leaped from the night upon her, its jaws ravening.

A stream of intense fire, like a firehose jetting lava rather than water, burst from the tip of the wand, completely incinerating the attacking wolf. The cloud of hot ash that was formerly the animal blew towards Tamara. She ducked aside and down, raising the wand just in time to destroy a second wolf.

The next few minutes were a frenzied time of blasting wolves, trying to avoid clouds of hot ash and general leaping about on, over and among the stones. One of which was blasted by the wand, the surface layer of rock glowing like coals in a perfect marshmallow toasting fire, before settling down to being intensely black with the stone half a centimetre thinner than it used to be, which Tamara knew was going to puzzle several ancient-monuments people of her acquaintance.

Nine wolves attacked in total. For quite some time after the ninth blew past her in ashen ruin, Tamara stood waiting for more, her wand ready, before she remembered the aggressor period allowed for only one attack in the first turn. Surely the wolves had been it, and another lot of wolves after half an hour would be a second attack?

She sat down then, with her back to her favourite and fortunately unburnt stone, and started shaking. Her clothes were dotted with tiny holes from sparks, and she had a slight burn on her neck, which she suspected was going to look embarrassingly like a love bite.

Furthermore, apart from the basic use of the Wand to incinerate wolves, the Knowledge had *not* grown in her head, or at least not meaningfully. She could feel there was a lot more to the Wand, but she couldn't quite grasp what it was. It was like trying to remember someone's name, and no matter how hard you tried, it was just out of reach. The Knowledge hadn't imparted anything beyond Flaming Jets of Lava 101. Nothing about *Them*, or how to find Arthur, or anything useful at all.

"Annoying old bat," muttered Tamara to herself, thinking of Blaise. She rubbed the burn on her neck and thought she ought to get home and put something on it. But all the leaping about had taken its toll, not to mention the lateness of the hour. She'd worked a full day at the dig before coming up to the Sheepstones, and she was exhausted.

"Fuck it," she whispered, and fell asleep against the stone.

Tamara woke just before the sun came up. She felt groggy and sore, and there was a light dew on her face. Her mouth and throat were dry, as if she had a hangover, and her right ear hurt. It took her a few seconds to work out she'd fallen asleep at the Sheepstones. In fact, leaning against one. She remembered watching the sunset, and had a vague recollection of chatting to someone – a walker, or a farmer – and then falling asleep, but nothing else.

Except the dream. A very detailed dream, that she now took several minutes to cement in her memory.

It concerned a party of post-Roman Britons, maybe sixth century. They were filling six very large pottery urns with treasure. They sealed the lids of the urns with wooden stoppers and a great deal of wax, and then buried them on the shores of a small lake or lough south of Hadrian's Wall, intending to come back and retrieve the treasure later. But she knew from the strange flip-forward and back nature of the dream that they were all killed, the last one years later on the shores of some icy, possibly Nordic country. The lough's shoreline changed, water encroached over the spot, and the treasure was completely lost.

But the men who buried the treasure
had taken note of the shape of the lough,
the skyline of the hills to the north
and the position of the sun in relation
to the hills. Tamara, as a disembodied
observer, had followed along. She could
superimpose the sixth century landscape
over the modern one, which was not
so different.

She knew the lough, though the water
level had ebbed back in the modern age.
Tamara frowned deeply. It was such a
vivid dream. She knew the exact place, it
would be about thirty feet from the shore
of the lough now, a hop and a skip from
the Stanegate, once a Roman road. The
treasure was astounding, both in terms
of archaeological and monetary value.
Hundreds of wooden cards, written on in

ink, records of some kind; silver vessels, including a highly decorated drinking cup; votive plaques; thousands of coins, both gold and silver; jewellery of all kinds; and numerous weapons, including many very fine swords, with jewelled pommels.

But it was only a dream. Or was it her archaeology-sodden subconscious speaking to her? Had she noticed something there when driving past one day, something that had lodged in her mind that had only just now worked far enough to the surface to provoke a dream?

Groaning, Tamara got to her feet and at that point discovered her clothes were pitted with tiny holes, and one of the stones nearby was inexplicably pitch black. She stared at the holes, then groaned over to the stone and touched it.

The black came off in crumbly pieces; it was like picking at a burnt sausage from a barbeque. She looked around, forehead severely furrowed. The ferns around the stones were broken and pushed down, and there were ashes everywhere, as if someone had flown over in a cropduster full of fireplace leavings and unloaded it all.

Her neck hurt too. Tamara used the camera on her phone to take a look. There was a burn there, a thick red line about as long and wide as her finger. And there was a weird heavy chopstick thrust through the belt of her Barbour shorts...

"What the fuck?" whispered Tamara to herself. Something very strange had happened here. She felt an incredibly strong urge to simply get away, and gave in to it. Dropping the chopstick, she set off down the path through the ferns, initially at a restrained walk, which turned into a run and then an all-out sprint to get to the Land Rover and a quick drive home to her studio apartment in Westgate Road, only resisting the temptation to speed where she knew there was a camera.

It wasn't until almost lunchtime that she felt relatively calm. A shower, another three hours' sleep, and a huge brunch had done its work. It was Saturday, so she didn't have to go into the university, and while there would be volunteers at the current dig, she wasn't rostered on to be there supervising.

The dream of the treasure burial stayed with her. At two o'clock she studied Google maps and other satellite images, searched ADS and other databases to see whether anything of archaeological interest had been found there, and discovered a total lack of any LiDAR coverage of that particular area.

At three o'clock, she couldn't resist any longer. She drove back out along the A69 towards Hexham, then on to the Stanegate, following it until she spotted Grindon Lough and pulled over. The site in her dream was near the eastern shore.

But there was nothing there to suggest any reason to dig. It was just undistinguished, marshy ground. The lough had definitely receded, probably in relatively recent times, but there was nothing to indicate this spot was any different to any other, or worth the time and expense of investigation.

Tamara went back home and called her supervisor, Professor Rob Collins, despite him being on holiday at his brother's house in upstate New York. The first minute was taken up with insisting she hadn't crashed the Land Rover nor done anything to any other departmental assets, but he was not much comforted by her urgent request for permission, and even worse, for him to begin the necessary paperwork for a dig at Grindon Lough, on no basis whatsoever except for what she called a 'hunch', as she chose not to refer to her dream.

"We simply haven't got the budget," he said. "Look, if you can get the money from somewhere, a grant or... or I don't know... run a Patreon or something..."

"I think it's urgent," said Tamara. She frowned, because this was a new thought. "Heavy rain might raise the level of the lough again, make it much more difficult. It's been a dry summer so far..."

"OK," said Rob. "We're about to go to dinner... uh... why not grab the gear from the department tomorrow and do a geophysical survey, say three or four grids of twenty-by-twenty metres size with both resistivity and magnetometry? That'll only take a day or two and make a big difference with any grant applications."

"Right," said Tamara slowly. Any delay felt like it was too long. "I'll do that."

"Let me know how you go. Of course, if you can get any money from anywhere, I'll back it, help you with the approvals and so on. But you'll have to do most of the paperwork."

"Yeah," said Tamara. "Thanks, Rob."

The call was barely disconnected before Tamara started going through her own and everyone else's lists of potential providers of grants or funding. Most of this was just crossing out ones that were already tapped out, or would take months if not years to respond.

But at nine o'clock, long after she should have stopped for dinner, Tamara found one of her archaeologist friends on Facebook referring to a grant she'd received to conduct a speculative dig of a potential late Roman villa in central

Turkey, from a source Tamara had never heard of: the Albert Levinson Jr Panomnisoft Foundation.

Tamara went down the Google rabbit hole and discovered Albert Levinson Jr had been an entrepreneurial software developer, an American turned into a dedicated Englishman like T. S. Eliot. He founded the (almost only) British software success story Panomnisoft. He had also been a keen amateur archaeologist, probably of the annoying and potentially damaging kind from the sound of it.

When Albert Jr died in 2005, his daughter Alberta Levinson took over and greatly expanded the business. While Panomnisoft itself meant little to Tamara, she recognised many of its subsidiaries, which extended across numerous different industries and were often household names. The application process for one of the Albert Levinson Jr grants was to send an email to AlbertGrant@panomnisoft.com attaching key details that took up no more than a page, and Alberta – who was many times a billionaire – would decide herself. The success rate, freely given, was one in ten thousand applications...

The email was sent at 4am, and Tamara collapsed into bed, failing to note that the strange single chopstick she had thrown away at the Sheepstones was now on top of a pile of overflowing books badly balanced on her windowsill, the foundation being *Thud!* and the topmost book *Bring up the Bodies*, the wand nicely illuminated by the moon shining through the glass.

Tamara spent the next few days on the geophysical survey, being strangely unsurprised to see substantial pits with very high magnetic readings, typical of results from other known hoard sites. Even better, the resistivity readings revealed flares, or hotspots, in the same positions as the pits. She forwarded these results to Professor Collins, who was much more excited, and to Albert grant email, resulting in a basic acknowledgment of the additional information.

The grant was approved four days later, the paperwork for the dig completed a mere twenty-one days after that, and within three days of commencing the preliminary work, the first urn was found, containing even more fabulous and important treasures than Tamara had seen in her dream. Her reputation instantly rose into the stratosphere, her work and the constant demands by the media grew even more all-consuming, so much so she totally forgot about the whole weird business with the Sheepstones and all that, and after a while she even managed to push aside the fact that it was a dream that had led her to what the Daily Mail Online shriekingly described as "the biggest archeological find since Carter stepped into Tutankhamen's tomb."

Five months later, Tamara woke up just after dawn on the morning of what was supposedly going to be one of the most important days of her life and knew that this was definitely true, but not for the reason she'd been expecting when she went to sleep.

This was because a silver-haired woman in a brilliant white suit was sitting on the end of the bed, rather like a cat that has snuck in during the night and found the best place for itself which also happened to be the most annoying for its host. She was holding a Ventolin inhaler and looking cross.

All of a sudden, Tamara remembered meeting Blaise before.

"Fuck!"

"Well you might say that. Every now and then the Knowledge doesn't take hold properly," said Blaise. "Which has totally set back our side, I can tell you. I really regret not choosing China over Britain, because their Monkey has already teamed up with Tripitaka and it's going swimmingly, whereas – stop that!"

Tamara froze in the act of picking up a very large and badly written historical reference book she'd been planning to read in bed and never did, but seemed exactly the right thing to hurl at this unwanted intruder.

"Put it down," instructed Blaise. "Very good. Now hold still while I apply the Knowledge to your other ear. Maybe it'll find a way into your thick head from that side."

Tamara struggled against the command but could not move. She remembered everything now, or as much as she'd been told, and if she'd been able to move a muscle she would have screamed in anticipation of the awful pain. But she couldn't. The next thing she knew her head ached as if from the worst hangover, the sun through the window indicated that dawn was an hour past, and the Knowledge had indeed found a way into her brain.

Blaise was still sitting on the end of the bed, reading a glossy magazine that wasn't in any language Tamara had ever seen and had a picture of something like a giant purple slug on the cover, posing to show off a utility belt. Or a slug corset or something.

"I hope it worked this time," said Blaise. She didn't sound very confident.

"Right. I'll be off. Remember, future of the world and all that."

"I have to steal *Alberta Levinson's* baby?" protested Tamara. An enormous quantity of constantly updating and shifting information was roiling about inside her head, most of it hard to pin down. But this one fact kept coming back to the surface. "I could get life in prison!"

"Unlikely," replied Blaise. "You'd have to be alive. *They* won't let you get away with that."

"But she's only just been born," continued Tamara. "What kind of person steals a three-week-old baby from her mum?"

"A Merlin kind of person, I'm hoping," said Blaise. "If it makes you feel any better, it was a surrogate birth. Alberta only supplied the egg."

"Of course it doesn't make me feel any better!" snapped Tamara.

"She hasn't even given the baby a name yet," said Blaise.

"So what!"

"Well, maternal attachment seems lacking—"

"I won't do it," said Tamara.

"What a disappointment you are," said Blaise. "Best Merlin candidate, forsooth! Well, *They* will finish you off anyway and I suppose in your dying moments – *They* are never that quick, *They* like a bit of torture and so on – you can revel in the fact that you could have saved the world and didn't, and all because you wouldn't steal a baby who needs to be stolen so she can grow up to be the Necessary Arthur. The Chosen One. The Hero who mostly fixes everything up."

Tamara looked at her mulishly. She could feel the Knowledge inside her head but it was fragmented, hard to grasp. Some things were easier to fix on than others, and it did indeed seem that the world was doomed if *They* won, and she herself would be an automatic forfeit, which meant death, as soon as the second round of the Game began. So steal a baby now or have slightly less than seven years to live and then die horribly...

"Who started this whole stupid game thing—"

But she was talking to empty air. Blaise had disappeared.

46

"Shit," muttered Tamara. She sat on the end of her bed with her head in her hands and wondered what the hell she was going to do. This was supposed to be the most momentous day of her life because in four hours' time there was going to be the biggest media blabfest the university had ever had, at the so-called "Grindon Hoard" site, where *Alberta Levinson* was going to announce a massive donation to build a dedicated museum and visitor centre, and Tamara was going to become an associate professor, vaulting above her peers.

Except that probably wasn't going to happen now. Because she was supposed to go and steal the benefactor's baby...

Tamara picked up the Wand. She suddenly understood that one of the things it could do was remotely control any computer, access any system, change data, and so on. With the obligatory warning that *They* might notice.

She pointed it at her MacBook and looked at how much the other graduate tutors at the university were paid. It worked instantly, secure pages flashing up in an instant, as if her broadband connection was suddenly a thousand times faster. Then she looked at her bank account, added a thousand and one pounds to her current account, and there it was…

"Shit," whispered Tamara. Everything was suddenly very concrete. "I suppose I do have to kidnap the baby."

She started with the information she could have got anyway, and then very delicately searched out a few key details that weren't available via any public search. After fifteen minutes, a plan began to form. Or not exactly a plan, more of a sort of cloudy gathering of the bits and pieces that somehow might go together into a plan. A pretty crappy plan, but it didn't seem likely any other kind might arise.

Tamara quickly discovered the workaholic Alberta Levinson, her three-week-old as yet unnamed baby daughter (so Blaise had told the truth about that), two nannies, two executive assistants, and five bodyguards had flown from London to Newcastle very early that morning on her Gulfstream G550 jet, transferred to an AgustaWestland AW139 Pininfarina Edition helicopter despite the fact it would be quicker to drive, and had gone on to a country house hotel called Avaunt Castle that was completely booked out for Levinson's party, at a mere £20,000 a day. The hotel was only five miles from the Grindon site.

According to the email between Levinson's assistant and the head of security which Tamara had just read (which she had the Wand make look like a Russian hacker prying) the baby, the nannies and two bodyguards were to stay at the hotel while Alberta, the assistants and the other three bodyguards went to the site for the media event.

"So," Tamara said to herself. "The media event is at eleven thirty. It's nine fifteen. I have to secretly get to Avaunt Castle, steal the baby but somehow so no one notices straight away, take her... somewhere safe... get back here, go to the media event, pretend nothing's happened."

She got out her field notebook and pen and almost wrote a list, beginning with "1. Get into Avaunt Castle" before stopping herself writing anything potentially incriminating. She put the pen aside and took up the Wand again, thinking about its capabilities. Frustratingly, the Knowledge still didn't seem to be working properly. She could feel information but couldn't access it, kind of like seeing the titles of books she could never open.

One thing was clear, while the Wand was an incredibly powerful device, using it risked attracting *Their* attention, particularly if it was to do with any connected technology, like the Internet, or phones. On the plus side, if *They* used their similar devices, Tamara would also be able to feel their presence.

"I know what you're getting for Christmas," she muttered to herself, and laughed, a very little bit. Clearly, the main lesson was that whatever... well, *magic...* she could do without... the safer it would be.

Yes said the Wand, in her mind.

Tamara jumped.

"I didn't... well, I suppose I did know you could talk," she said. "I mean I do now... but I didn't a second ago... this Knowledge thing doesn't seem to be working properly."

It seems not. There's too much information to actually fit in your brain at any one time, the Knowledge is a quantum-entangled interface to a much larger data repository located in an interstitial dimension. When you need to know something, it should be there. But it has not initialized in your head properly.

"Oh great," replied Tamara. "So I have to think about what I need to know before I can possibly know I need to know it? And it isn't working properly anyway?"

That is correct.

"Great. Listen, do I have to carry you around as a stupid chopsti – ah, I see not. That worked. For once."

How would you like me to physically manifest? Or embed, I can be like an extra appendix or a small lipoma—

"No! I know. How about a ring? My favourite, from Rosemary Sutcliff's books, that got me into Roman history in the first place. The Aquila family ring, gold with the flawed emerald and the dolphin carved into—"

Yes. I have the reference. How about this?

The chopstick wriggled in her hand, bending up until its ends met and it became a hoop, which shrank swiftly and became much heavier and more dense, the white plastic that wasn't actually plastic turning into gold. A slightly smoky emerald emerged in the bezel, there was a spark of intense light, and a dolphin was etched in the gem.

Tamara put the ring on the second finger of her right hand. It was slightly loose, but it tightened up to be just right. She held out her hand, admiring it.

"Well at least this is unequivocally a good thing. Now, I can't call you the Wand anymore..."

I am still the Wand, no matter my shape. As the Knowledge is the Knowledge, wherever it resides.

"I'm going to call you Dolphin. Dolph for short."

I suppose it's better than Wanda.

"You do dad jokes?"

I am a sophisticated entity. As the Knowledge will tell you.

"Well it isn't telling me anything. Piece of crap."

It is true Blaise was using a, shall we say, third-hand applicator.

"This just gets better and better. She gives me a hard time for not being the best possible Merlin. I bet she's a terrible player in this Game of yours."

Her syndicate is ranked in the lowest one percent. Of the thirteen million, seven hundred and eleven thousand, three hundred and eighteen syndicates in play.

"That good? Why did she have to choose me!"

You really must be the best candidate to be Merlin.

"Great. And yes, the one thing I am getting from the Knowledge is that the world does need an Arthur, or it will in due course, and I've got to get her."

So how are you going to steal the Necessary Arthur?

"You tell me."

That I cannot do. You wield the Wand, the Wand does not wield you.

Tamara sat and thought, occasionally shaking her head and sighing.

"I'm an archeologist," she complained to the Wand after about ten minutes. "Not a career criminal. Or some sort of spy or whatever."

You have a practical mind, oriented to problem solving.

"I guess."

She got up and made a cup of tea, sipping it as she paced backwards and forwards.

"I know where to take her. I guess Blaise picked me for that, or that was part of it. But I have to get her first."

One step at a time is a time-honoured procedure for maximizing the chance of success.

"Hmm... I've got to get into the castle... you can transform things, right, but it works best if they are already like what they need to become? Otherwise *They* might notice?"

Yes. Is the Knowledge working for you now?

"Off and on," said Tamara, scowling.

Transformation uses less notional energy than creation, in most cases.

"Notional energy?"

It shouldn't exist, but it does. Perhaps I should also point out that I am not fully charged.

What!

I am afraid Blaise requisitioned me from the incorrect outfitting stream, inward, not outward. I have been recharging but that takes two full orbits of the sun, I am at less than a quarter charge.

"What does that mean?"

The Knowledge will inform—

"The Knowledge isn't telling me anything! Okay, okay. I need a disguise, how much power will this take..."

She went to the kitchen cupboard and pulled out a white-stringed mop head, and from her wardrobe a fancy dress fake beard, legacy of a Viking party from a long-ago undergraduate excursion to York.

"Can you turn these into a proper-looking fake beard and hair, not too long, that I can wear? How much power will that take?"

Yes. This is trivial, requiring less than one seventy-third of my existing charge. Actually giving you a real beard and hair, or making you physically male would take one eighteenth of my charge. A power use which would possibly attract Their *attention.*

"Okay, that's okay. Better than… well, you make me some hair while I see what Barry left behind."

Barry was Tamara's ex-boyfriend, who'd joined Sea Shepherds and gone to the southern hemisphere to defend whales. Or, as was actually the case, to chase after a Norwegian reformed whaler. He'd left most of his clothes behind. Quickly she sorted out some basic khaki trousers and shirt, and a green anorak, which all together looked kind of official.

"Now I need an ID card for, uh, I don't know... oh yes, thanks Knowledge for once... The Environment Agency. Can you make one, Dolph?"

"Yes. Best if you sketch one on a piece of card, though. Again, the smaller transformations, from as near like to like, are best."

"OK."

Tamara quickly drew a picture of the ID card the Knowledge had put in her mind. Almost as quickly as she sketched, the lines firmed and became printed and sharp, her circle with two dots and a line for a mouth became a picture of her face, even the paper turned into some kind of plastic laminate.

"A long-haired, bearded inspector from the Environment Agency," she said. "Oh, I'd better do up some forms. What would they... oh yes... electronic these days. Make my iPad look right. Thank you."

Her three-year-old iPad in its weathered nylon case melted and reformed into a brand new one in a leather folder with impressive logos, and the device was pre-loaded with forms for reporting all kinds of transgressions and disasters.

The mop became an excellent wig of dreadlocked black hair, which she put on and pulled down and was surprised by how good it looked. The beard and moustache had some sort of static property that kept it fixed to her skin, which she initially found alarming since it was quite hard to pull off. But it also looked good. Together, they said "wildness tamed for official reasons". Once Barry's anorak was on to disguise her shape, Tamara looked entirely like a male counterculture type tidied up for government work.

"So what would I be looking for?" she mused to herself, and then smiled. "Hey, can you make a big Geiger counter out of a little one?"

Certainly.

"And a proper gas mask out of a face mask I use for dust?"

Yes. Though there is an increased chance of detection the more I do of this sort of thing.

"And I'll need some coveralls turned into an anti-radiation suit. Is that too much, I mean would use up too much power?"

These are all trivial applications and will amount to less than one fourteenth of my charge. But even tiny uses of notional energy can collectively become detectable.

"Right. Well, you can do it on the way. So if it is detected, we'll be on the move.

That is wise.

Tamara gathered everything she needed into her backpack, then sidled down the stairs and out the laundry door of her block of flats, sped across the communal garden and through the hole in the fence into the lane. A few blocks away, Dolph found a non-descript green van that had not been driven for a month and so presumably would not be quickly missed. He opened the doors and started it for her, and just like that they were off to Castle Avaunt.

Along the way Environment Agency decals blossomed on the doors and amber lights grew on the roof.

They drove past the dig site, which was already swarming with media vans. The roped-out car park was full and many fancy Range Rovers and late-model vehicles were parked along the Stanegate. As Tamara expected from reading the security arrangement emails, halfway from Grindon Lough to Castle Avaunt they passed a convoy going the other way, two huge Bentleys preceded by two police Vauxhall Corsas and followed by two more, plus a rather massive black armoured car the police must have borrowed from the Met.

There were also armed police officers on the gate to the hotel's long driveway, which they'd blocked with their Land Rover. Tamara had expected this and Dolph had cautiously gone into the Northumbria Police IT systems to prepare her story.

Even knowing this, Tamara could barely stop her hand shaking as she stopped well short of the police vehicle, lowered her window, and held her ID card out.

"Morning," called out the police sergeant who approached, not that close, the words and smile rather in contrast to his full body armour and the assembled equipment dispersed upon his person, which Tamara could see included a radio, mobile phone, telescopic baton, Glock 17 self-loading pistol and Taser X26 conducted electrical device. Not to mention the Sig MCX carbine slung across his front, from which his hand didn't move, his finger perfectly disciplined outside the trigger guard.

"Morning," replied Tamara laconically. Dolph had temporarily lowered her voice, it sounded really weird and she almost looked around to see who else was talking. The officer read her ID carefully, and then looked at the iPad Tamara held out so he could see the Google map of the hotel with a cross-hatched red area marked behind the castle.

"I'm checking up on possible radioactive contamination. Got a report there's a whole lot of radium paint, got buried here after World War II. This place was a barracks back then."

"You can't go in today," said the sergeant. "Got a VIP visiting. Well, VIP's family right now."

"Yeah, well, they'll be a radiated VIP family if there really is five hundred litres of radium waste buried somewhere close by," said Tamara grumpily. "My boss said she called you lot yesterday."

"Five hundred litres?" asked the sergeant. "Is that a lot?"

"Enough to give everyone within two miles of here cancer if the barrels have rusted and that shit's leaked out," said Tamara. "Worse if you're closer. I was just going to park here and get into my suit."

"Yeah, right," said the sergeant, slightly uncomfortably. He looked at his fellow officer, a woman, who while she must have heard gave no sign of it on her steely face. She just kept scanning the road. "If something like that was buried here they'd have found it years ago."

"You reckon?" asked Tamara. "Well, like I said, I'm supposed to go check and my boss said she already told you lot, all the paperwork's done."

"Yeah? Wait here."

He went back to the Land Rover, muttering something to the woman officer as he went past. She shook her head, but slowly shifted closer to the road and farther away from the castle.

He's calling the dispatcher, they'll find your visit logged in to go ahead from the duty inspector last night. Yes, he's got the go ahead.

Tamara let out a sigh.

"By the way, can you stop me being shot?"

Up to a point. If both these officers shoot at you with those carbines, from different angles, probably not.

"Good to know."

The sergeant came back.

"Yeah, we were supposed to be told you were coming, and it can't wait," he said. "Uh, you reckon we're all right here?"

"Probably," said Tamara. Time was getting away. "I'll just pull up a bit farther away... I mean farther on and suit up, OK? Any more of your lot up at the hotel?"

"No," said the sergeant, shaking his head. "Private security, though... I'll give them a call, let 'em know you're coming."

"I don't have to go into the hotel," said Tamara. "The site's round the back. Tell them to stay clear. Stay inside, keep the windows shut. It's probably nothing, but..."

"There's a baby up there," said the female officer, coming back from the road. "Should we..."

"It's probably nothing," reassured Tamara. "I'll know in an hour or so, maybe less. No need to do anything yet."

Hastily, she did a U-turn and drove the van about fifty yards away, reinforcing the desirability of distance, parked it on the shoulder, and jumped out to quickly don the radiation-proof suit, which was bright orange and kind of puffy and had a massive clear domed plastic hood. She left the hood hanging down her back, put the gas mask on but pushed it up on her forehead and hefted the imposing Geiger counter Dolph had embiggened from the cheap little DX-1 detector Barry had paranoically given her for use on her Black Sea late Roman villa dig, because he'd heard a Soviet nuclear submarine had sunk nearby.

She swung the detector about as she walked back, the officers pretending they weren't listening to its tack-tack-tack drumbeat and weren't watching the flashing lights. Both flinched as Dolph made it emit a sharp electronic whistle.

"What's that?" asked the sergeant nervously.

"Low battery," said Tamara. "Nothing here, I mean nothing out of the ordinary. You call them up there?"

"Yes. Look, as soon as you know anything, call me okay?"

Tamara nodded and made a fuss of taking his mobile number.

"I reckon it's nothing," she said, giving the lie to her words by immediately pulling down her mask, lifting up her hood and completely sealing her suit. Her muffled voice now sounded rather like a recorded official warning, muffled and almost incomprehensible.

"Don't let anyone else in until I get back. Unless it's like half a dozen HazMat crews..."

It was hot in the suit and mask, trudging up the drive. The castle was actually a Victorian folly aping a fourteenth-century square tower, but it had been beautifully restored, as had the gardens around it. The whole place looked lovely, and expensive. Tamara wasn't surprised that as she passed the front a woman in a grey suit that screamed "hotel manager" came running out.

"Just go back inside, please," Tamara called out, her voice very muffled. "It's probably a false alarm but best everyone stay inside for now."

"What?" asked the woman, coming closer. "What is this about? That policeman at the gate said radioactive—"

"A large quantity of radioactive material may have been buried here at the end of the Second World War," said Tamara as loudly and clearly as she could. She kept lumbering on, clumsy in the puffy suit, the manager tripping along next to her. "Please stay inside until I have completed my tests."

"But that's ridiculous, how could—"

"This place was owned or run by the MoD wasn't it?" asked Tamara. "Look, stay inside will you? You are legally required to comply with my directions."

"Yes, all right! But please be quick. We don't want our guests alarmed."

Tamara waved and kept going, around the side of the castle and over to the cottage which served as one of the hotel's suites, which she'd seen on Google Maps. It was empty, she knew from reading Levinson's assistant's emails. Quickly she went around the back, out of sight of the castle, and got out of the suit and gas mask, wig and beard.

"OK, fix the gas mask with the wig and beard inside the hood, animate it and send it out on some sort of search pattern, back and forth."

I hear and obey. But this is a slightly higher order of, well I suppose it is best called magic. The probability of detection increases a little.

"Do it."

Her voice had gone back to normal, Tamara noticed, though she hadn't ordered Dolph to make it so. Perhaps it had been connected with the wig and beard…

The puffy orange suit rose up of its own accord and picked up the Geiger counter. Tamara suppressed a shiver as it marched back into the view of the castle windows and began to sweep the Geiger counter backward and forward. Though it was her own idea, a living, moving radiation suit was just creepy.

"Is anybody watching the left side of the cottage? CCTV?"

I have looped all the video surveillance. One of the bodyguards is at an upper window, watching the radiation suit. If you run diagonally to the kitchen door, there is a good chance you will be unobserved.

Tamara ran. At the kitchen door, she stopped.

"Anyone in there?"

The chef and an assistant are prepping for lunch, they are facing the south side. If you crawl swiftly they should not notice.

Tamara got down low, pushed the door open and listened. She could hear knives chopping and a discussion of sport or something like that, it was too indistinct to be sure. She didn't hesitate, but went down on her hands and knees and crawled straight through the kitchen, paused to listen for a few seconds at the swing door to the dining room before she went through.

Guided by Dolph, she made it to the fourth floor undetected. This was where the largest suite was, currently inhabited by the two nannies, the two bodyguards and the baby, the girl who would be Arthur.

"I want you to mess with their minds," whispered Tamara. "The bodyguards and the nannies. I want it so they don't notice me, they think the baby's asleep, everything's fine. I know this will probably alert *Them*, but I can't think how else to do it. Uh, I guess you'll have to do it to everyone in the building. Can you make it so they just go on for an hour or so and don't notice anything?"

Probability of detection approaches certainty if I do this.

"Yeah, so *They'll* know I've done something here. But how quickly can they react? And they can't attack me directly, right?"

Not without cheating.

"What! They can cheat? I mean *They* can cheat?"

There are penalties. But yes.

"This is the stupidest fucked-up Game. Who... oh come on, the Knowledge isn't going to tell me..."

While you may not know the principals, you should know the Game has kept an overall... I suppose you might say cold war or lukewarm peace in the seven galaxies these last ten million years. Only five civilisations have been totally eradicated in that time. If there was war instead… well, the Game is to be preferred.

"If *They* do cheat, what can *They* do?"

A wide variety of actions are possible.

That's helpful. How long have I got?

We might have five or six minutes from when I act.

"Shit."

Tamara took a very deep breath.

"Okay," she said. "Do it."

Four minutes later, she was climbing over the low stone wall that marked the boundary of the hotel's land with the farm next door. Baby Arthur… Arthura… Aretha maybe… was asleep in her astonishingly heavy car capsule, strapped in and professionally nanny-wrapped in flannel. The baby's go bag was over Tamara's shoulder.

Tamara was aiming for a barn she'd noted from her Google Maps reconnaissance. It had cars parked outside in the photo, and she was hoping that they'd be there today.

They *know. Attention on hotel spiking. Ah…*

"What?" gasped Tamara. It was hard going across the ploughed field. She could see the front end of a fairly decrepit Land Rover on the other side of the barn, but hopefully there was something better still out of view.

They've taken control of the anti-radiation suit. Obvious, I suppose.

Tamara looked behind her. The puffy orange suit was climbing the wall. It didn't stand up once it was over, it got down on all fours and began to sniff about like a dog.

No human senses. Following our energy trail. Me, in other words.

Tamara rounded the corner of the barn, and just managed to avoid colliding with a very surprised farmer.

"Hey, oop!"

Tamara's ringed hand tapped his shoulder.

"Sleep!"

Dolph did whatever it did, and the farmer folded up under her hand.

Tamara jumped in the Land Rover. Dolph started it at the same time, the engine ragged. Aretha started to cry, a piercing sob. Tamara put the capsule down on the floor on the passenger side.

"Stick the capsule down, protect her!" she yelled at Dolph.

The gear shift was recalcitrant, but she slammed it into first and wasn't gentle with the clutch. The vehicle lumbered forward, just as the radiation suit came scuttling around the corner of the barn, still on all fours.

Tamara put her foot down and drove straight into it.

There was no jarring impact. One second the suit was there and then it wasn't. Tamara kept her foot down and pointed the Land Rover at the track that led to the road, shifting up into second.

There was a scrabbling, drumming noise underneath Tamara's feet.

It's under the vehicle, holding on.

Tamara steered off the track into the drain on the side, the Land Rover bucking, hoping this would scrape off the suit underneath. She spun the wheel and the Landie skidded back to the track.

Puffy, orange hands appeared outside the windows on either side of her and began to pull down the glass.

"Kill it!" screamed Tamara.

They're pouring power into it, it will take most of my—

"Kill it!"

There was a bright flash and the smell of ozone. All the instruments on the Land Rover's dash suddenly indicated zero or empty, though it kept going. Benefit of ancient technology.

Will take most of my remaining charge.

Tamara glanced in the rear-view mirror. There were shreds of orange along the track behind her, emitting wafts of blue smoke. She slowed down to negotiate the grid at the farm gate and to look out for traffic, before turning onto the road.

"Is it dead? Have they lost us?"

It's neutralised. It had limited senses so they probably do not know who they're looking for. But They *will now know who you have chosen to be Arthur.*

"Shit. I wanted more time. Will you be able to unlock and start another car for me?"

Yes. But little more.

Aretha was still crying, but it was not full-on screaming, just dissatisfied sobs.

Two miles along the road, they swapped the Land Rover for a bilious green Fiesta parked at a layby where a popular footpath started. As Tamara carried the baby capsule over, Aretha decided it was time to start full-on screaming again.

"Ssshhh," said Tamara ineffectually as she put the capsule in the backseat. "Dolph, fix the capsule here."

Done.

"And the screaming? What do I do about the screaming?"

I could make her unconscious. But with the young there is a small risk of brain—

"No! Ah, damn, we can't wait he maybe she's hungry."

Tamara opened the go bag. There were two bottles of prepared formula in an inner cool compartment. She got one out and held it to Aretha's mouth, who immediately started to greedily suck.

"Can you hold the bottle? I've got to drive."

Yes. But I have only one ninety-eighth charge remaining.

Tamara leaped into the front seat. The car was already going, thanks to Dolph. She strapped in and headed out. Behind her, the bottle in the baby's mouth shifted down a bit, to ease the flow.

"Her own personal ghost nanny."

I've had worse jobs.

Half an hour later, Tamara drove the Fiesta into a layby along a forested section of the road. Aretha was asleep again. She picked up the capsule and the bag, crossed the road after checking there was no traffic and walked a hundred yards to where a bridlepath began, that rose up a low hill.

Aretha woke up and at first seemed inclined to scream again, before deciding she liked the bouncing she got from Tamara struggling uphill with the capsule. She was quiet, though bright-eyed, and her little hands clenched and unclenched at unseen things in the air.

"She isn't actually seeing anything is she?" asked Tamara anxiously.

Not that I can detect.

They left the bridlepath to take a rougher footpath along and then down the other side of the hill, into a dense wood of oak and ash. There, it rejoined a very narrow, not-quite one-lane road that while tarred, clearly saw little traffic. Tamara trudged along it for another hundred yards until she came to the farm gate, and the sign.

A word etched in faded pokerwork on a slab of wood stuck on an angle on the gatepost. It said "Yána," which Tamara knew meant 'refuge' in Elvish. *Lord of the Rings* Elvish.

Tamara opened the gate. A string of bells that hung on it tinkled, though she also noted the plastic owl in the fork of the nearest tree had a video camera eye that was tracking her, and she knew there were other sensors and alarms.

The track beyond wound up through the ash forest, with just the peak of the main house visible, with its curiously large satellite dish. Yána was a sort of commune, composed of mostly retired scientists with slightly techno-anarchic leanings, and its leaders, though they would deny being leaders as such, were Tamara's aunt Helen and her partner Lorileigh Lyon, who had bought the place with the money from the Nobel Prize for Physics they'd shared twenty years before.

Briefly, Tamara wondered what she should tell Aunt Helen and Lorileigh, and the others in the commune, before she realised that the best and most effective thing would be to tell the truth. She'd have a terrible time stopping them experimenting with the Wand, or trying to… but it would be best.

She'd only got halfway to the house when Helen came hurrying down the path.

"Tamara!" cried Helen as she got close, her arms extended to hug niece and an unexpected but certainly delightfully beautiful sleeping baby in the capsule. "And baby! Why do you have a baby, Tamara?"

"It's complicated," sighed Tamara. "And I will explain in detail later. Right now, I need to leave Aretha with you, borrow some clothes and your car and drive like a fiend back to my dig for the whole official celebration."

"That's today?" asked Helen, who was inspecting Aretha. Though an enormously distinguished scientist she was never very good with dates. "Who does little Aretha belong to?"

"It's complicated," repeated Tamara. "Keep her hidden and I will explain everything. I'll be back with all her proper documents... uh, new documents. And some tech for you to drool over."

Helen raised her eyebrows. Tamara raised her ring.

"It's very complicated, but also I think you'll find very interesting," she said. "Dolph... um... do something that looks amazing and won't use much power."

So specific. All right. But then I will have to go dormant, until I can be recharged, under the moon.

Another Tamara suddenly flickered into existence next to the original, but this one was made of golden light. She bowed, turned into a fountain of golden sparks that formed characters and spelled out some incredibly complicated formula and disappeared.

"Hmmm," said Helen. She blinked quickly six times, a sign of acute interest.

"Magic ring," said Tamara.

"Obviously superior technology," said Helen, with a sniff. "And so of course, I am *very* interested. But more importantly, are there nappies in that bag?"

"Yes. Why?"

"Clearly you have not had your sense of smell technologically enhanced," said Helen. "Come on. Lorileigh is the most adept at baby changes. And she has the best clothes."

Half an hour later, Tamara parked her aunt's BMW at Hexham railway station, leaped out and collared the one taxi that usually lurked there, the driver appearing to be astonished anyone wanted his services. Shortly thereafter, he delivered her to Grindon Lough. Now properly attired in a Nobel prize–winner's deep navy pants suit and with her own ID, she easily made her way through the cordon of police and university PR people to her place in the front row inside the huge marquee erected for the occasion.

"Where have you been?" whispered Professor Collins. "I've called you four times!"

"Lost my phone, overslept," Tamara whispered back. "Everything okay?"

Clearly the news of the kidnapping had not broken, because she could see Alberta Levinson sitting across the aisle, looking at her phone, surrounded by guards and flunkeys. She looked bored, not distressed.

"Just a bit behind schedule, but it would have been good for you to meet Levinson before we started... ah..."

He was interrupted by an executive-looking woman who had come over from the other side of the front row. A very attractive, super-competent type, holding two iPhones in her left hand. She smiled.

"Hello," she said. "I'm Ms Levinson's principal executive assistant. You must be Dr Tafika?"

"Yes," said Tamara, smiling back. She felt an immediate, powerful attraction to this woman, but she was puzzled as well, because the emails she'd read had been from a principal executive assistant who was male, or at least that's what she remembered, David or Dave... and as per usual the Knowledge was not reminding her...

"I am Ms Elzein," said the woman. "But please call me Nimue, we'll be working a lot together."

Tamara kept her smile fixed and hoped the sudden caution she felt did not reach her eyes as they shook hands.

"Great!" she said brightly.

"Oh, what an interesting ring!" said Nimue. Her voice was musical, the tone of it seeming to resonate inside Tamara, as if her whole body wanted to shiver in answer.

Tamara didn't want to let go of Nimue's hand. But she did.

"Yes," said Tamara. "It's a replica of a Roman ring. From one of my favourite historical novels."

It's going to be a tough seven years, she thought to Dolph. *And that's only getting to turn two!*

I have faith in you, Dolph replied, his mental voice very faint and distant, *Merlin*.

About the Author

Garth Nix is a New York Times bestselling novelist. More than six million copies of Garth's books have been sold around the world, they have appeared on the bestseller lists of *The New York Times*, *Publishers Weekly*, *The Bookseller* and others, and his work has been translated into 42 languages. He has won multiple Aurealis Awards, the Ditmar Award, the Mythopoeic Award, a CBCA Honour Book, and has been shortlisted for the Locus Awards, the Shirley Jackson Award and others.

More dyslexic friendly

titles coming soon...

BOTH
PUBLISHING